The First Gift

For Maximilien Lafrance Liebman—M.L.

KAR-BEN PUBLISHING
A division of Lerner Publishing Group, Inc.
241 First Avenue North
Minneapolis, MN 55401 U.S.A.
800-4KARBEN

Website address: www.karben.com

Library of Congress Cataloging-in-Publication Data

Gadot, A. S., 1944–
    The first gift / by A.S. Gadot ; illustrations by Marie Lafrance.
        p.   cm.
    Summary: As a boy tells about the first gift his parents gave him, his name, he identifies someone else who had the same name, recalls how names came to be, and lists different names one person might be called. Includes facts about Jewish naming customs.
        ISBN-13: 978–1–58013–146–9 (lib. bdg. : alk. paper)
        ISBN-10: 1–58013–146–8 (lib. bdg. : alk. paper)
        [1. Names, Personal—Fiction. 2. Jews—United States—Fiction.] I. Lafrance, Marie, ill. II. Title.
    PZ7.G11716Fi 2006
    [E]—dc22   2005003704

Manufactured in the United States of America
2 – CG – 4/15/2010

The First Gift

BY A.S. GADOT

ILLUSTRATIONS BY MARIE LAFRANCE

KAR-BEN
PUBLISHING

Once there was a child
whose name was David.
But...

His mother called him **Davey,**

His father called him **Son,**

His brothers called him **Useless,**

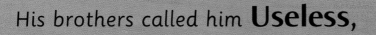

His harp teacher called him **Genius,**

The kids on the block called him **Red**
(for obvious reasons),

And his teacher often called his parents, because, instead of studying, he spent his time shooting stones with his slingshot.

When this child grew up, he became a king.
His people called him King David,
and whenever they addressed him they said:

"Your Majesty."

But his son Solomon
just called him **Daddy.**

Where do names come from?

The first name in the world was Adam.

When God finished creating the earth and the sky,
the moon and the sun, the plants and the animals,

God created a man and called him **Adam.**
Then God showed Adam all the wonderful
and amazing things that had been created
and told him to give them names.

And Adam did. He named all the animals and
all the flowers. Even the very small ones.
And these were good names.

Many children have names
that come from the Bible,…

…names like
Joseph

and
Sarah,

Noah,

Ruth

and **Rebecca.**

Children in different countries have different names...
In Mexico children are called

Jose, Carlos, Juanita, and Maria.

In Russia, they are called

Nicholas, Boris, Natasha, and Svetlana.

In Israel they are called
Noam, Gal, Yael, and Tamar.

The very first gift my parents gave me was my name.

It was totally, absolutely mine,
but everybody used it all the time.
It was a gift I couldn't see, I couldn't touch, but I could hear.

Even though I'm not a king, they named me David after my great-grandfather.

But, I, too, have many names.

My baby brother calls me **Dave-Dave.**

My savta in Israel calls me **Dah-veed,**
my Hebrew name.

My friends call me **Red,** for obvious reasons.

And my teachers call me in from recess
when I want to keep playing.

When I grow up I might also be called
Doctor or **Rabbi** or **Coach**

or even
Mister President.

And maybe someday I'll have a son,
but he'll just call me **Daddy.**

Jewish Naming Customs

Traditionally, Jewish children are named for a beloved family member. Ashkenazi Jews (those of German and Eastern European descent) generally name their children after someone who has died, to honor that person, and to keep his or her name and memory alive. Sephardic Jews (those of Spanish and Portuguese descent) have a tradition of naming their children after both living and deceased relatives.

Baby boys receive their names at the circumcision ceremony (*Brit Milah*). Baby girls are often named when a parent is called to the Torah in synagogue or at a naming ceremony (*Simchat Bat*).

While some families give their children only a Hebrew name, many give their children two names: a secular or "everyday" name, as well as a Hebrew name that is used for religious rituals such as being called to the Torah. Sometimes the secular name is a translation of the Hebrew name: *Ya'akov* becomes Jacob, *Chanah* becomes Hannah. In other instances parents choose a name that starts with the same letter as the Hebrew name. *Shira* becomes Susan and *Baruch* is Brian.